To the children of Wales who loved hearing this tale – E.M.

For the bundle of joy that is Finlay – P.H.

ABOUT THE STORY

This folk tale, found in Wales, Ireland, India, eastern Europe and north Africa,
may originally have been linked to the ancient Greek legend of King Midas.
Asked to judge between the music of Apollo's harp and Pan's flute,
Midas unwisely chose Pan – and furious Apollo cursed him with ass's ears.

The King with Horse's Ears copyright © Frances Lincoln Limited 2003
Text copyright © Eric Maddern 2003
Illustrations copyright © Paul Hess 2003

First published in Great Britain in 2003 by
Frances Lincoln Limited, 4 Torriano Mews
Torriano Avenue, London NW5 2RZ
www.franceslincoln.com

British Library Cataloguing in Publication Data
available on request

ISBN 0-7112-1957-5

Set in Berling

Printed in Singapore

1 3 5 7 9 8 6 4 2

The KING with Horse's Ears

ERIC MADDERN

illustrated by PAUL HESS

FRANCES LINCOLN

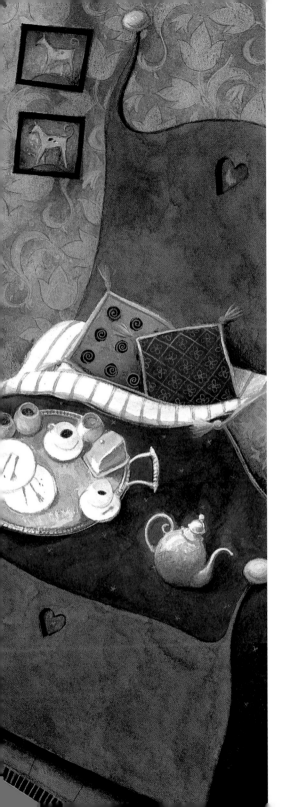

King Mark was a good king. Everyone loved him. But he had a secret hidden under his hat – an embarrassing secret. He had the ears of a horse.

The king was so ashamed, he kept his ears covered with a silken cloth and wore his crown jammed down hard.

No one knew about the ears except for one person – not the queen, as you might expect, but someone else who got close to him.

It was …

… his barber!

Once every six months the barber came to cut the king's hair, and of course he saw the horse's ears, plain as two witches' hats. But King Mark said to the barber, "If you ever tell anyone about my ears, I'll have your head off in the morning."

The barber didn't want to lose his head in the morning or at any other time, for that matter.

But secrets are peculiar things. They want to be told, and they gnaw your insides, they twist in your tummy, they poke and pester you. If you can't tell them, you get ill.

And that's what happened to the barber. He got such a dreadful stomach-ache that at last he had to go to the doctor.

The doctor examined the barber's tongue, took his pulse and checked his reflexes. Finally he said, "I'll tell you what the matter is: you've got a secret! What you must do is tell your secret to someone."

"But I can't!" shouted the barber. "I'll lose my head."

"What you must do," said the doctor, "is tell your secret to the ground."

"To the ground?" echoed the puzzled barber.

"Yes," replied the doctor. "To the ground."

So the next day the barber walked through
the town, across the fields and into the
forest, until he came to a clearing with
a little stream flowing through it.

"This is just the place to tell my secret,"
he thought. He made sure no one was
listening, then knelt down, took a deep
breath and whispered,

"King Mark has got . . . horse's ears!"

He looked around again. No one
was there, so he said it again, a little louder
this time: "King Mark has got horse's ears!"

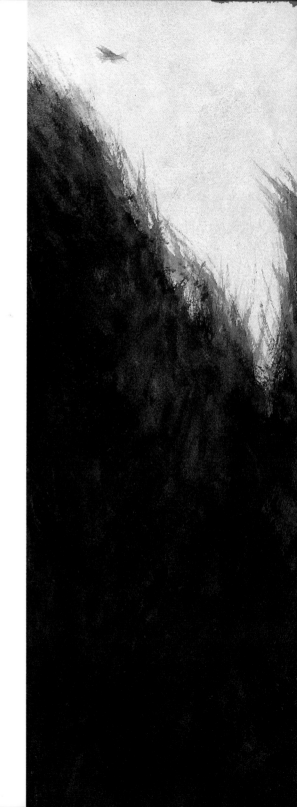

He was starting to enjoy himself, so he said even louder:

"King Mark has got HORSE'S EARS!"

Then he jumped up and began dancing around, singing,

"King Mark's got horse's ee-ars,

King Mark's got horse's ee-ars,

King Mark's got horse's ee-ars!"

He felt much better, as if a great weight had been lifted from his shoulders. He skipped and hopped and danced all the way back to the castle, and never gave the king's secret another thought.

But the next day, in the place where the barber had told his secret to the ground, some tiny green shoots appeared and began to grow.

They grew all through the day and the night into strong, straight, beautiful reeds, the finest reeds in the land.

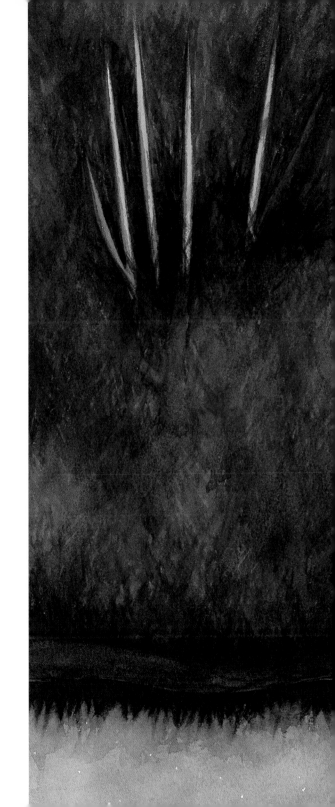

A few days later, a band of travelling minstrels were going through the forest on their way to King Mark's hall. They stopped to eat their bread and cheese. Afterwards, one of them took a stroll and came upon the reeds, the finest he'd ever seen.

Now, he was a pipe player and made his pipes out of reeds. So he cut some down, went back to his friends and they spent the afternoon cutting and whittling and making a brand new set of pipes. Then they went on their way to King Mark's court.

That night the king held a great banquet. Lords and ladies came from all over the land and the tables were groaning with food. When the feasting was over, the king clapped his hands.

"Bring on the musicians – it's time for the dance!"

So the minstrels took up their places. The piper stepped forward with his brand new pipe to play the king's favourite tune. He put the pipe to his lips and began to play.

Oh dear! What came out was not the king's favourite tune, but,

"King Mark's got horse's ee-ars,
King Mark's got horse's ee-ars,
King Mark's got horse's ee-ars."

The king's face went red with embarrassment. It went white with rage. It went black with fury! He called his guards and bellowed, "Throw them in the dungeons! I'll have their heads off in the morning."

But the piper was a brave man. He stepped forward.

"Your Majesty," he said, "it's not our fault. It's the pipe. It's bewitched."

"Bewitched?" roared the king. "Here, let me see." He took the pipe and examined it. Then he remembered that he could play a tune or two himself. So he began to play. But once again, what should come out but,

"King Mark's got horse's ee-ars."

Then he snarled, "Bring me the barber!" and the poor barber was dragged in front of the king.

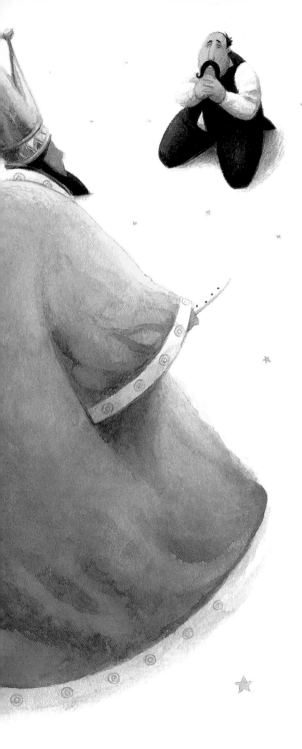

"I didn't tell anyone, I promise I didn't," sobbed the barber. "It's just that I had this terrible stomach ache and the doctor said I should tell the secret to the ground ... so I told the secret to the ground ..."

"To the ground?" bellowed the king.

"Yes, Your Majesty, to the ground."

Well, after that the whole story came out.

And by the time it was out, well, it wasn't a secret any more. Everyone knew.

But the strange thing was, no one laughed. And even stranger was, the king felt different too. A great weight had been lifted from his shoulders. He didn't have to worry about his secret any more.

Then someone called out, "Your Majesty, may we see your ears?"

"My ears?" replied the king, doubtfully.

"Yes please, Your Majesty."

"Very well," said the king, and he took off his crown, unfurled the silken cloth, and there were his horse's ears, for all to see.

Then the king walked around the hall showing off his ears, and everyone clapped. And because he was the only king in the world with horse's ears, and because he was their king, they were proud of him. And because they were proud of him, he was proud of himself.

After that, the king had a new crown made with two special holes for his ears to poke through. His ears were much happier, and so was the king. He lived a good long life and when he died, his story spread all around the world.

So, if you have something unusual about you, don't be ashamed, be proud. Just remember: *you* are the only one of you there is!